This book belongs to

_____

_____

For Sebastian,
with thanks for all his help.

First published in 2000 by
David & Charles Children's Books,
Winchester House, 259-269 Old Marylebone Road,
London, NW1 5XJ

Text and illustrations © Charles Fuge 2000

The right of Charles Fuge to be identified
as the author and illustrator of this work has been
asserted by him in accordance with the
Copyright, Designs, and Patents Act, 1988.

A CIP record for this title is
available from the British Library.

ISBN: 1 86233 217 7 hardback
ISBN: 1 86233 305 X paperback

Printed and bound in China

Yip! Snap! Yap!

By Charles Fuge

David & Charles
Children's Books

Woof!

Woof!

Rruff!

Barking Dog
1 Barking Lane
Barking

Then turn the page
and make more noise
and do some doggy stuff!

Dinner time for greedy dog . . .

Curl up with
a sleepy dog . . .
Hrumph!
Zzzzz!

Phew!

Careful of the guard dog . . .

Gruff!

Grrr!

G-Ruff!

Don't catch fleas from itchy dog . . .

Scritch! Scratch! Scruff!

Yip! Snap! Yap!

Pant!
Slurp!
Lap!

Follow trails with sniffer dog . . .

Sniffle!
Snaffle!
Snoo!

Barking dog,
Growling dog,
Munching dog,
Snoring dog,
Sniffing dog,
Panting dog,
Itchy-scritchy-scratching dog,
Yapping dog and
Puppy dogs howling
at the moon . . .

Scratch!

Aroo!

Yap!

**Other David & Charles Picture Books
for you to read and enjoy:**

Sometimes I Like to Curl up in a Ball
VICKI CHURCHILL • CHARLES FUGE
hardback: 1 86233 253 3

A Cuddle for Claude
DAVID WOJTOWYCZ
hardback: 1 86233 262 2

Little Ones Do!
JANA NOVOTNY HUNTER
SALLY ANNE LAMBERT
hardback: 1 86233 230 4

Not Me!
NIGEL MCMULLEN
hardback: 1 86233 209 6

David & Charles
Children's Books